THE FURY'S VENGEANCE

An Urban Fantasy Thriller [Novelette]
(Myth & Magic, Book 3)

S. W. Millar

TAGLINE
PUBLISHING

Tagline Publishing

ALSO BY S. W. MILLar

Myth & Magic

The Thief's Magic # 0.5 (FREE prequel short story)
The Witch's Revenge # 1
The Coven's Executioner # 2
The Demon's Shadow # 4 (out in May 2022)
More *Myth & Magic* coming soon...

The Fury's Vengeance: An Urban Fantasy Thriller [Novelette] (Myth & Magic, Book 3)

Copyright © 2022 by S. W. Millar

All rights reserved

Published by Tagline Publishing

https://swmillar.com

ISBN (eBook): 978-1-915192-05-9

ISBN (Paperback): 978-1-915192-10-3

Cover design by Damonza

Formatted using Atticus

contents

IS THIS BOOK FOr YOU?

This book contains adult themes, fantasy violence, and colourful language. Basically, all the fun stuff. I write using British English. Sound good? Then read on and enjoy!

For Granny and Poppa. Poppa, I wish you were still here to read my words on the page.

"Revenge is an act of passion; vengeance of justice. Injuries are revenged; crimes are avenged."— **Samuel Johnson**

CHAPTER 1

Thump, thump, thump, thump.

The noise launches a hand grenade into my dreams and blasts them to pieces. I wake sprawled on my side on the sofa, a pool of dribble under my cheek. "Ugh." I drag a hand across my mouth and smack my lips. What is that fucking sound? I crack my heavy eyelids open and glare at the huge digital clock hanging over the fireplace.

The scarlet numbers glare back.

Twenty to three in the morning.

I shoot the clock the finger. Is it mad to fight with inanimate objects? Probably. Do I give a shit? No. I bury my face into the cushion and take a deep breath through my nose. The woody scent of oud—spicy, sweet and smoky—floods my senses, and a slow warmth spreads through my abdomen and my mouth kicks up at the corner. Even after five years, the smell of my wife's perfume still makes me hornier than a bitch in heat.

Someone bangs on the door again, louder this time.

Who the fuck is that? I wriggle onto my back and prop myself up on my elbows. "Babe. Someone's at the door."

No response.

"Maria?" Ice prickles the length of my spine. "You want to get that?"

The house is still.

I sit up and swing my feet to the floor. Where is she? She should've been home hours ago. I'd returned home from food shopping around early-afternoon, cleaned the house, vegged on the sofa for a minute, and... I must've dozed off. Despite the normalcy of the day—a day in the life of a stay-at-home-wife—something feels off. "Maria?"

The chime of the doorbell makes me flinch.

A knot tightens in my chest and my fingers, stiff and shaky, comb the sofa for my phone. I thumb the power button and Maria's grinning face fills the screen. No messages. She always tells me if she's going to be late. My stomach twists. I tap Maria's number. It rings and rings and rings. "Pick up, come on, pick up."

The answerphone clicks in. "*You've reached Detective Inspector Maria Green-Hernandez. I can't come to the phone right now, but—*"

I disconnect the call and the room sways.

The letterbox creaks open. "Tally?" A low, gentle, female voice I recognise. "It's me and Christian."

That's Tori.

Christian and Tori.

Why the hell are they here?

This late.

When two detectives from the Magical Investigations Department show up at your door unannounced—especially in the dead of night—it never means anything good.

Christian and Tori work for Maria.

Did my wife send them here?

If so, why?

I—

"Open the door, Talitha," Christian says, his voice sounding flat and tired.

My mouth goes dry.

I've known Christian for a long time—ever since he started reporting to Maria—and he only calls me 'Talitha' when he has something important to tell me.

You've reached Detective Inspector Maria Green-Hernandez. I can't come to the phone right now...

Something in my stomach swims about, making me feel queasy. "Er—okay—just coming."

Open the door, Talitha.

Goosebumps erupt on my skin.

Don't panic.

Stay calm.

It might not be anything bad.

"Give me a sec." I stand, straighten my neon green vest top and ripped jeans, tug on my biker boots, rush to the door. My fingers tremble too much to twist the key in the lock. I point at the latch. "*Recludo.*" Magic tingles along my arm. The lock clicks and the door swings open.

Christian hovers on the porch, fingers fidgeting with the dark knot of hair fastened at the nape of his neck.

Tori stands next to him, wearing floaty trousers and a loose, daffodil yellow jacket. As always, her full lips bow in a natural upward curve, giving the impression she's about to break into a grin. Her eyes, however, are downcast. "Hi, Tally."

"Hel—" My voice cracks. I clear my throat, plastering a bright smile on my face "Hey. It's not that I don't love seeing you, but it's a bit late for a social call, isn't it?"

Christian's fingers still at the back of his head, the colour draining from his cheeks.

You've reached Detective Inspector Maria Green-Hernandez. I can't come to the phone right now...

My breath catches, but I keep my smile wide.

Tori blinks.

Just once.

Real slow.

Christian reaches into his pocket, pulls out his warrant card, and flashes it at me.

I've seen it hundreds of times before. The letter's MID stamped across the top in bold, light blue ink, the passport-sized photo of Christian scowling into the camera, the plain white background.

There's something wrong with it, though.

His job title.

The badge should say, "Detective Sergeant, Christian Winter."

But it doesn't.

Instead, it reads, 'Acting Detective Inspector, Christian Winter'.

You've reached Detective Inspector Maria Green-Hernandez...

There's an odd flutter in my belly.

That's not right.

Acting.

Detective.

Inspector.

Each word strikes me like a hammer blow, harder every time.

Tori says, voice soft as puppy-fur, "It'll be better if we do this inside."

"I—" Dark spots cloud my vision. I brace my hand against the door-frame. "Better if we do what inside?"

Tori glances away.

"Christian?" I ask, my voice an octave higher than usual.

His face crumples.

I can't come to the phone right now...

"No." I shake my head. "Christ, no."

He glances up, his eyes shimmering with tears. "I'm so sorry, mate."

CHAPTER 2

A weight drops into my stomach and drags me to my knees, and a wounded animal screech scrapes past my teeth.

Christian steps over the threshold, crouches, and pulls me into a tight hug. His fingers skim my hair and he makes gentle shushing noises. His sandalwood scent washes over me. I breathe deeper, hoping the familiar fragrance will comfort me.

It doesn't.

Maria bought him that aftershave for his birthday.

Maria.

Christian's shoulder muffles my screams and his black coat soaks up my tears.

I cry for a long time.

Christian's still murmuring words of comfort into my hair, but their meaning doesn't filter through.

Minutes or hours or days, I can't be sure how long the tears last.

"I'm sorry," he says again, with an air of desperation. "Fuck. I'm sorry."

I squirm, struggling to push him off me.

He doesn't budge, his strong arms squeezing tighter.

I relent—I don't want to, but I do—and sob until my tears run dry.

Eventually, Tori says, "Christian, we should get her inside."

I sniff, a thick, wet sound. "How did she die?"

Christian draws back from our crouched embrace, dark eyes boring into mine. "Tori's right. Why don't we go in?"

I grip his arm tight. "How?"

"On the job."

"Someone... killed her, you mean?"

I want him to say no. That it was an accident or something, but instead, he says, "We really should go in." He peers around at the neighbouring houses. "Don't want to attract any unnecessary attention."

By *unnecessary* he means mortal attention.

Witches might live alongside mortals, hiding in plain sight, but we don't like them to examine us too closely.

The threat of exposure.

Of some kind of modern-day Witch Trials...

Even in my grief-stricken state, the thought makes me shiver.

I take the... *deepest*... breath and, when I exhale, all the air shudders out of me.

Christian rises, and I rise with him on rubber legs. "Come on," he says, quiet.

I nod, mute, and let him guide me along the hall, back through the sitting room and into the kitchen.

The front door clicks shut and Tori follows us.

Christian perches me on a stool at the breakfast island. "You need something to take the edge off."

It isn't a question. He knows me too well. Way too well. Let's just say he knows I like a drink and leave it at that. "You know where the gin is," I say, the hollow voice sounding nothing like mine.

He flicks the lights on and rummages around in the cupboards. "Tonic?"

I snort, prop my elbows on the breakfast bar and knead my eyelids with my palms. "I hate drinking alone, so help yourselves."

"Can't." Tori perches on the stall opposite mine. "We're on duty."

Prissy bitch.

Heat floods my chest and my fists clench. "Just have a *fucking* drink."

She blinks again, another of her slow blinks, and her face falls.

The heat seeps away as quickly as it came, leaving the room icy.

What the hell was that?

I rake a hand through my hair and gather it up so that it hangs over one shoulder. I can't apologise—that's not really my style—but I need to say something. "You didn't deserve that."

"It's fine, honestly." She reaches across the breakfast island, rests her hand on mine and gives it a light squeeze. "I can't even imagine what you're going through."

She's right.

She can't.

I yank my hand away as if her touch shocks me and try to ignore the queasy way my stomach rolls. Tori is all warm brown eyes and consoling smiles.

I, in contrast, am a stone-hearted mega-bitch.

Christian places a glass tumbler on the granite worktop in front of me with a clink. "There you go, bud. Get that down you."

I drain it in one.

The neat gin scorches on the way down, but in a good way. I hold the glass out and shake it at him. "Same again."

"I want you to calm down, not pass out."

"Who are you, my mother?" Stupid thing to say. My mother would be the last person to refuse me a drink. "Less talking, more pouring."

"That's not a good idea."

"No. It's a marvellous idea."

He accepts the glass with some reluctance.

Tori runs a hand through her thick Afro curls, brushing them behind one ear. "You look so happy."

"What?" I narrow my eyes at her.

What the fuck is this dumb bitch talking about. Happy? Is she—

Tori inclines her head towards mine and Maria's wedding photo.

I force the vicious, alien thought from my mind. "Oh, yeah. It was her idea, to wear black." I bite my lip, accept my refill from Christian, and take a huge gulp. "I wanted to go the traditional route for once. Guess what she said." I pause. "'Screw that bullshit patriarchal notion of female purity.' Told me she'd rather die than—"

The resulting silence sucks all the air from the room and leaves me dizzy. My stomach lurches. "Fuck." I slide off the stool and stagger to the sink on wooden legs. I gag and hinge forward. A thick stream of hot vomit spews from my mouth and splatters against the white porcelain. My eyes sting with tears and I spit to get rid of the foul taste and wipe my mouth with the back of my hand.

Maria's gone, and she's never coming back. This realisation punches me hard in the gut. I want to talk to her.

Want to hear her voice.

Want to wrap my arms around her and squeeze and never let go.

The last words we spoke to each other drift through my mind, as insubstantial and fleeting as smoke on the wind.

Does this top look okay?

Maria. It looks like all your other black tops.

Charming.

It looks fine.

I can hear your eyes rolling.

Seriously, babe, it looks okay.

You're not even looking.

Don't need to, because it looks fine.

Sometimes, I wish you paid more att—

Scoot! You're going to be late for work, then Kate the Destroyer will harvest your ovaries and turn them into earrings.

Oh, Jesus. She's not that bad, Tal.

Sure.

It looks fine.

That's the last compliment I gave her... if you can call it that. They were the last words I ever said to her.

I should've said she looked beautiful, or gorgeous, or sexy as fuck, because she does.

She... *did.*

Silent tears stream down my face.

"That's it." Tori pats my shoulder. "Let it out."

"I—love—loved her so much." I force the words out between broken sobs.

Tori's gentle pats continue. "You must be heartbroken."

Heartbroken.

Stupid fucking word.

My heart isn't the problem.

It's my gut.

Someone has plunged a knife into my intestines and is twisting, twisting, twisting. I need to know. Don't want to, but *need* to. It's like a hunger, an ache that won't go away until my earlier question gets answered. I straighten and shrug Tori's hand away. "How did it happen?" My voice is cold, accusatory.

A crease appears between Tori's eyebrows. "I'm sorry, but we can't tell you. It's classified."

Stupid cow.

I don't mean that.

Do I?

I turn away from Tori. "What happened, Christian?"

He sets his jaw. "You're putting me in an awkward position."

"I don't give a shit." I jab a finger at him. "She was my wife, and I know you had your professional differences, but she was your friend. Tell me what happened."

A heavy sigh escapes him. "We were—"

"Christian, you can't," Tori says in a warning tone.

He lets out a long sigh. "I have to. I can't lie to her."

"Kate said—"

"I know what she said and, if she asks, I'll tell her it was my decision."

Tori opens her mouth and, for a second, I'm convinced she's going to argue, but then she purses her lips and makes a zipping motion over them.

"You sure you want me to tell you?" Christian asks.

I fold my arms and arch an eyebrow.

"Fine." He straightens his black and white checked tie. The words tumble out of him in a rush. "We were trying to apprehend a criminal called Dylan Carmichael—"

"Wait. That name rings a bell. Dylan Carmichael? As in Maria's old boss, Carmichael. She said he went AWOL. She said—"

"It's a long story. Short version. He went rogue. He was the head of a Supernatural Organised Crime Group called COVEN. We tracked him to an abandoned house, and he... and he mesmerised all his followers. He—" his voice breaks "—I can't. I can't do this."

"*You* can't do this. Are you fucking kidding me? *You* can't do this." I lean back against the worktop and grasp the edge, hard. "Tell. Me. What. Happened."

Christian's eyes are glassy. "Carmichael instructed one of his followers to kill Maria using a death-strike, and they shot her in the chest."

I clench the worktop so tight my knuckles ache. I'm overcome with the sudden urge to hurt someone, to maim someone. "And this *follower*, the one who murdered Maria—"

Christian scratches his chin. "They didn't murder her, Carmichael did. They were under a spell."

The heat in my chest races up my neck and into my cheeks. *Traitor.*

That's what Christian is.

That word, applied to Christian feels so wrong, but he's defending Carmichael's actions. He's—

Tori steps forward and rubs my back in small circles. "I get this is hard."

I want to scream at her.

Hard.

Something caustic and bitter has taken up residence inside me, like the news of Maria's death brought with it something malevolent. More malign thoughts scream into the void my mind has become.

How dare you? You come into my home and rip my heart out with a pair of rusty pliers and all you can say is, "I get this is hard." You don't have a fucking clue, you patronising bitch.

I grip the worktop harder and harder and harder and—

Crack.

CHAPTER 3

A web of hairline fractures spreads across the granite beneath my fingertips.

Tori steps back. "Tally?"

"How did you do that?" Christian stares at me with wide eyes.

How indeed? I hadn't cast anything. I prise my fingers off the cracked granite and they shudder. "I—I'm not sure."

"Shit. What's going on?" Christian says.

I narrow my eyes at him. Something loosens in my head and, when I speak, the words are so cold they sound like they're uttered by a stranger. "I'll tell you what's fucking going on, you insensitive prick."

His brow furrows. "Tally...I—"

"Well, it's true. What else would you call a man who brings his fucking girlfriend over to tell his *best friend* that her wife's been murdered? Rubbing your perfect relationship and your perfect life in my face. Some mate you are."

The quiet that follows is all consuming.

I get that funny slipping sensation in my mind again and... oh, Jesus. I clap a hand to my mouth. "I don't know why I said that."

Christian looks like I punched him in the nuts.

Good. He's lucky I don't tear them off.

"Shut up," I say.

Christian looks from me, to Tori, and back again. "I didn't say anything."

"No. Not you. It's like... it doesn't sound like me."

"What doesn't?"

"The..."

What was I going to say?

My thoughts.

The voice inside my head.

Christian and Tori exchange worried glances.

Tori holds her hands out, palms down. "Stay calm. It's going to be fine."

I grit my jaw so hard my teeth hurt and fiery rage boils in my gut.

Something snaps.

"No, it isn't!" I spin back round to Tori and smack an open palm into her chest.

Her face creases in pain. She screeches and flies backwards, sailing through the air as if tossed by the wind. Her body strikes the opposite wall, and she crashes to the ground, bounces once, and lays still.

My outstretched hands shake.

A beat passes, a withheld breath, and another.

On the third beat, Tori's chest rises and falls, but she doesn't stir.

"Jesus." Christian sprints past me, races over to Tori, and collapses to his knees by her side. "What did you do, Tally?"

"I just... I pushed her. That's all. I didn't mean to—"

His eyes meet mine and they widen.

"Why are you looking at me like that?"

His Adam's apple bobs up and down. "Your... hair."

"What about it?" I snatch a handful of my hair and hold it out.

It's streaked white, and—what the?— my cuticles have darkened to an unhealthy grey. My heart pounds, and a patch of sweat forms between my shoulder blades. "What the hell is happening to me?"

Christian's face is pale.

"Christian?"

"I know what this is. Shit. I—I didn't think it was real." He whips out his phone. "We need to act fast. Kate's still at work, she'll know how to fix this."

"No." My voice is firm, and it's the one that doesn't sound like mine.

"You don't understand what's happening. We need to—"

"I don't give a shit."

"What?" His mouth puckers like the word tastes sour. "We need to fix this."

I quirk an eyebrow. "Fix it. Fix it? Why the hell would I want to fix it?"

"What do you mean?"

My scalp tingles. "I want to *use* it."

I flex my fingers, my arms. For the first time since Christian and Tori showed up on my doorstep and ruined my life like the selfish, good-for-nothing bastards they are, I feel...

Strong.

Whatever's happening, there's power to it.

Power more devastating than any magic I'd ever wielded.

Raw.

Untamed.

Like a hurricane, or a raging storm, or a...

A vengeful God.

Whatever it is, it's bottomless.

Endless.

It's speaking to me now.

Use me.

Use you how?

Against him.

Who? Christian?

Against the one who stole Maria from me.

Now, there's a thought.

But—

And on Christian too, if he gets in my way.

But only if he gets in my way.

I speak, using my cold voice again. The powerful one. "This follower of Carmichael's. The one who killed her. Where can I find them?"

Christian shakes his head. "He—"

"Ah, so it's a he, is it?"

Christian's lips form a tight line. "Why do you want to know where he is?"

"I want to make him a friendship bracelet." I roll my eyes. "Why do you think?"

"No." Christian stands. "This isn't you talking. That's what I've been trying to say. This thing that's happening to you. It's called Fury Syndrome, and it's clouding your judgement."

Fury Syndrome?

But that's... it's an old wives' tale.

An old memory surfaces.

A conversation I had with Crawler... God, there's a name I haven't thought about in years. Anyway, it was back when things were—well, it was before Maria.

CHAPTER 4

BEFORE MARIA

Crawler and I—Crawler isn't his real name, but people like us, people who slip through society's cracks, don't use real names—walk along Daxbridge canal, our ratty backpacks containing everything we own, which doesn't amount to much, slung over our shoulders.

"Hey, I forgot to tell you," Crawler says, a glint in his eye. "I bumped into this old witch dossing in that abandoned warehouse on Kendall Street."

I roll my eyes. "Shocker. Plenty of people squat there."

He clicks his tongue, pushing his fingers through his long, unwashed hair. "We got chatting, and he reckons he saw a Fury once."

"A what?"

"A Fury."

"What are you on about?"

"You must have heard about Fury Syndrome".

"If I had, I wouldn't be asking, would I, you bell-end."

"Point taken," he chuckles, then his expression sobers. "Story goes Fury's are witches who lose their way."

"Lose their way. How's that?"

"It's rare—like one in every God-knows-how-many-people-rare—but when someone a witch loves gets murdered, if the witch experiences really intense grief, magic can mutate."

I laugh. "*Mutate*. You've been reading that scratty *X-Men* comic again."

"It's a graphic novel, not a comic. I'm not twelve." Crawler huffs, deep in his throat, then continues. "You want me to tell the story or not."

"Whatever. Nothing else to do."

"Right. Well. They say—"

"*They?*"

He shoots me a look.

I pipe down.

"They say when magic mutates, it causes Fury Syndrome. It turns witches into Furies."

'Course it does mate.

I don't say this out loud.

Crawler's pissed off enough already.

I just listen as we pick our way along the canal path.

"First the witch gets these mood swings, then they lash out, then they start to change."

"Change?"

He bobs his head. "They lose their spell casting abilities, but they get, like, mad-crazy strength. All their senses get jacked up. Sight, hearing, taste, smell, touch. All heightened. Apparently, they're eyesight's better than any Sighted witch, and they can hear a heartbeat from a mile away. Their hair goes dead white, their irises go dark red—like dried-blood—and they've got these wicked-sharp black talons. In one of the stories I heard, they even have this super-powerful scream that can blast through objects... and even spells."

Despite the heat of the day and the sun beating down on the crown of my head, I shiver. "That's bullshit."

He shrugs. "Not according to the witch on Kendall Street. Want to know the weirdest bit?"

Yes!

I love a good story—especially creepy campfire-style stories like these—and it's been a long, long time since I was around someone who cared enough to tell me one.

I don't tell Crawler that.

Instead, I say, "Can't wait," my tone dry.

If he registers the sarcasm behind my words, he doesn't comment on it. "Furies who are in the middle of mutating get obsessive about killing the person who wronged them. Their change from witch to Fury is only complete when they've murdered the murderer."

Cold still permeates my skin. "You mean, like, they can't control themselves?"

He nods. "They basically go mad. Doesn't matter if there's an argument for not killing their target, they just keep going."

The cold intensifies. "Wouldn't they want to get better, though?"

"Not according to the legend. The Fury Syndrome makes them want to become a Fury." He waggles his bushy eyebrows and stretches out his arms in a zombie-like motion. "*Join us.*"

I laugh, shaking off the icy chill, saying, "Nah, I still think it's bullshit."

Crawler just chuckles.

CHAPTER 5

NOW

"**D**id you hear what I said, Tal?"

Christian's question brings me back to the present. "What?"

"Your judgement is clouded."

Furies who are in the middle of mutating get obsessive about killing the person who wronged them. Their change from witch to Fury is only complete when they've murdered the murderer.

"Quite the opposite." A small smile curves my lips. "Things have never been clearer. Where is he?"

"Don't do this. Don't let it control you. You'll lose everything."

I laugh, humourless, high and cool. "I've already lost everything."

Christian sets his jaw. "I can't let you do this."

"You can't *let* me." I jerk back as if he slapped me. "Maria's dead and the person who killed her is out there just walking around."

"No, he isn't. We arrested Carmichael, he's in custody."

"What? No." I pinch the bridge of my nose. Christian's right. Carmichael killed Maria, not the witch he mesmerised, it wasn't his fault and—

No.

What?

The follower fired the spell.

Christian said they didn't know what they were doing.

They killed Maria.

It wasn't their fault.

The follower has to pay.

It was Carmichael, he—

They have to die.

He has to?—but he wasn't in control; he didn't—

Enough!

The Fury's right.

I need to kill him.

I need to get revenge.

If I kill him, this pain will stop, it will stop, it will stop. My body shakes as my mind splits in two. I massage my temples with my fingers. "Shut up. Shut the fuck up."

"Don't listen to it," Christian shouts over my cursing.

"I don't—"

Give in to the rage.

Give in to the fury.

You know you want to.

"No, I don't." I'm practically screaming now.

If you do, it'll make you better. The agony will stop. You'll be able to think about Maria without—

My stomach clenches, stabbed by a sharp ache.

Without that.

"I'm going to call Kate," Christian says.

"I'm fine." The pain in my abdomen spreads to my chest and I double over, sucking in a breath through my teeth.

"You need help." His thumbs dart across his phone's screen.

The sharp stabbing migrates to my throat, a hollow burn that threatens to choke me.

I need to stop him.

I open my mouth wide... and scream.

The sound is deafening, like a thousand fire alarms blaring in unison.

Christian bellows in agony, his phone slips from his fingers, and he clamps both hands over his ears.

I scream until I'm breathless. I scream until my throat is raw.

He sinks to his knees and collapses to his side.

I run out of breath. My ears ring with quiet. I tilt my head towards the mirror on the opposite wall. A shock of white streaks strip my hair of colour and my nails are tar-black, and have lengthened. They taper into long, needle-like points.

Christian and Tori lie side-by-side.

They could be sleeping.

My limbs are heavy in a way they've never been before.

What have I done?

The answer stalks towards me and claws its way inside me.

You did what you needed to do, and you will again.

Yes, I will.

I stalk out of the kitchen, towards the front door, and grab my leather jacket off the peg. "If you won't tell me who he is, then I'll find someone who will."

CHapter 6

I skulk in a shadowy corner, my heart pounding.

The underground car park is dark and almost deserted, but a few cars remain, and the acrid stink of dried piss and mildew pollutes the air, the stench more familiar than I'd like. It reminds me of tattered sleeping bags, frostbitten fingers, and police shining blinding torches in my face.

A life before.

Before Maria.

Before the shy smiles, and soft kisses and the 'I love yous.'

My stomach twists and I swallow the bile scalding my throat.

A fluorescent light twitches and flickers above a set of lift doors in a burst of restless energy.

I know the feeling.

Still, I bide my time, the only sounds my breathing and the blood rushing in my ears.

I hate—

Ding.

The lift doors whisper open and *she* struts out, shoulders back, chin tilted upward. Everything about her is fierce. Maria says that—*said* that. I ignore the pinch in my chest. Yeah, she's fierce, all right. The confident stride and the severe trouser suit, the bright spark in her eyes that signals her keen intelligence.

DCI Kate Denton.

I trace the edge of my new claws with my thumb.

Well, bitch, maybe I'm fiercer than you now.

Kate's progress falters, and she halts, her entire body stiffening as she grips the leather straps of her handbag so tight that her knuckles turn white. "Who's there?" Her voice is smooth and rich, the rounded vowels hinting at a private education.

Stuck-up cow.

She waves her hand. "*Revelare.*"

I know the spell. A parlour trick used to reveal something hidden with magic.

Nothing happens.

Kate removes her thick, black-framed glasses, rubs her eyes and slides them back into place. "Get it together, woman." She straightens and stalks towards a grey *Audi*, her back to me.

Now's my chance. I flatten myself against the wall and dart around the car park's edge. My eyes never leave her.

She fishes about in her bag, searching for her car keys.

I slip behind her, snake an arm across her waist and crush her back to my chest.

She yelps, a sharp sound, and the handbag crashes to the floor.

A delicious tingle races through me. "Hello, Kate."

She recovers fast. "Whoever you are, I'd advise you to reconsider this course of action before you do anything rash. We are in a building full of MID officers, and—"

I shove her away.

She stumbles forward. Her hands fly out and slam into her car window.

I cover the distance between us in three long strides. My arm slithers around her waist again. I lean in close, my lips brushing her ear. "You speak to all your friends like that?"

Her expression—reflected in the glass—is so comical I almost laugh.

Almost.

Her lips part, eyes bulging. "Talitha? Is that you?"

"What, you don't like the makeover?" I pout in mock-disappointment. "I'm offended."

Her breath hisses through her teeth. "You're becoming a Fury."

"Tell me something I don't know."

She fastens a hand around my arm and chants an incantation.

"Ah, ah, ah." I bring the tips of my claws to her throat and dig in, hard enough to dimple the skin, but not enough to break it.

Her body goes rigid and the words die on her lips.

"*I'd advise you to reconsider your course of action before you do anything rash*." I slather my voice in honey, imitating her earlier words and her cut glass accent.

Kate scowls. "I'm not afraid of you."

I chuckle. "Liar."

All their senses get jacked up. Sight, hearing, taste, smell, touch. All heightened.

My nostrils flare.

Beneath Kate's perfume—something expensive and vanilla-sweet—is a salty tang of fresh sweat that makes me giddy.

I whisper. "I can smell your fear. You reek of it."

She swallows, the skin on her throat snagging against my claws. Beads of blood well up, trickle down her chest, and between her cleavage—copper taints the air. "What do you want?"

"The name of the bastard who murdered Maria."

"Didn't Christian tell you? It wasn't his fault, he was—"

"Did he kill her or not?"

"Technically, yes, but—"

"Then give me his name."

In the reflection, her eyes flash. "No."

I twitch my fingers and more blood flows. "Sure about that?"

"Consider what you're doing. I know you're hurting. I know Maria—"

"Don't you dare." I disengage my claws and clamp my hand round her throat. "Don't use her name against me like a weapon."

Kate makes a choking noise.

My grip relaxes. "Tell me his name, or I swear, I'll crush your windpipe."

"You can attempt to intimidate me all you want, I refuse to tell you."

Cold fury burns at my core.

How can I make her tell me?

Wait.

She has a family.

Can I go there? Can I resort to that?

The answer is clear before the question even forms. "How's Andy?"

Her back stiffens, ramrod straight. "You wouldn't."

"And Sally? Still enjoying college?"

"You bitch."

I smile, a thin smile, sharp as a blade. "Sticks and stones."

"I'm warning you. If you so much as breathe near my family, I'll—"

I grab her arm and wrench it behind her back.

Her shoulder crunches and she screams.

"You're not in a position to make threats."

Tears stream down her face. "Please, leave Sally out of it. She has nothing to do with this."

Her pleas cut through everything.

My pain, my grief, my rage.

My Fury.

"No!" I thrust her away.

She crumples to the ground, clutches her arm and groans.

I pace back-and-forth and twist my fingers together.

What would Maria want me to do?

She'd want revenge.

I spin on my heel and knead my temples. "She wouldn't want me to lose myself."

I pivot again.

She'd want justice.

And again.

"She'd want me to grieve."

One final spin.

She'd want that bastard dead.

Kate—who has stopped whimpering now—mutters something under her breath and flings out her hand.

A streak of silver light darts towards me.

I dash to the side, faster than I would've thought possible.

The glowing dart whistles past me and slams into the wall with a sharp *crack*.

She fires another.

I duck.

And another.

I dodge.

Kate screams in frustration.

I laugh. "Maria always said you were so strong, but you're weak. Your pathetic magic will never stop me."

Oh my God.

Why am I talking to Kate like this?

Because she's standing in my way.

She's my friend.

She's an obstacle.

"Stop," I croak. "Just stop."

Kate watches me with a wary glint in her eye, like I stand on the edge of madness and am about to tip over. She hauls herself to her feet. Her face drains of colour and she grits her teeth. Sweat dots her forehead. "It's not—ow—not too late. This can still be reversed."

"Can it?" My cuticles itch, and my talons retract a little.

She nods. "If we act now, yes."

Pain, hot and acute, stabs into the pit of my stomach, the back of my throat stings and my vision blurs. "I can't cope without her."

"You will, given time."

"I want her back."

"I know."

Sharper and sharper, and sharper still.

I can't handle it.

I want it to stop, and there's only one way to make that happen.

Give in to the Fury.

"Talitha." Kate takes a tentative step forward. "Fight this."

Don't listen to her.

"I can't, I'm not strong enough."

"Yes, you are."

Being strong is over-rated.

Give.

In.

Make it stop.

Make it all go away.

"I'm not." I shake my head. "You don't know me as well as you think you do. I've been fighting my entire life, and I'm tired, really fucking drained. The only time I stopped fighting—the only time I could—was when I met her, and now she's gone, and I've got nothing left to fight for."

Kate reaches out, fingers extended towards me. "Please, come inside. I can cure this. If we get enough liquid silver inside you, then—"

I flinch back and scrunch my eyes closed—an image of Maria's face burned into my eyelids. "I want the pain to stop."

"It will, if you let me help you."

I bite my lip. "I don't deserve your help."

Make it stop.

Give in to the Fury.

Make it stop.

The last of my resistance crumples, and I do as I'm told.

I give in.

CHAPTER 7

A dam bursts open within me, and I cry out.
Icy water floods my chest, my limbs, my brain. I let it fill me up, from the tips of my toes to the crown of my head. The biting cold numbs the pain and I welcome it. When it's over, I lean forward and place my hands on my knees. A curtain of hair falls across my face. Every single strand is pure white.

The pain has vanished.

I'm numb, save one thing.

A single-minded focus.

A thirst that needs to be quenched.

Vengeance.

I straighten and lift my hands, which are plaster-pale, with dark veins criss-crossing beneath my skin. My claws have doubled in length—they're razor sharp and harder than diamonds.

Kate gasps. "Oh, my God."

"Not quite." My voice is flat and emotionless.

"We still have time, we can—"

"Change the fucking record."

"Please, I—"

"I'm only going to ask you one more time." I take a deliberate step forward.

Kate scuttles back.

I savour the shiver of excitement that runs down my spine. "Tell me the name of the fucker who killed Maria. Tell me where he is, or I promise you, the next time you see your daughter, she'll be in a body bag."

"Okay. Okay. I'll tell you, but you have to swear you'll leave Sally alone."

I carve a slow X over my left breast with my index finger and smile wide enough to show all my teeth. "Cross my cold, coal-blackened heart."

She opens her mouth, closes it again and presses her lips into a thin line.

"I'm waiting. I hate waiting."

Her lips part. "His name is—"

The air rips and a flash of bright violet light blinds me, and I lift a hand to shield my eyes as a fierce hot-cold wind whips my hair back and makes my clothes snap against my skin. The wind dies down, the light fades, and the air reeks of burned ozone.

I lower my hand.

Christian stands between me and Kate, his eyebrows creased into a scowl.

"Christian, where's Tori?" Kate says.

"I had to portal her home after what Tally did."

Kate glowers at me. "What did you do?"

"She's fine, it's just a mild concussion," Christian says.

I clench my fists and jab a pointed talon at Christian. "Portalling here was a big mistake."

He raises a hand, fingers splayed, and pointed at my chest. "This ends now."

"That's not fair." I stick out my lower lip and waggle a finger at him. "I'm only just getting started."

"I don't want to hurt you, Tal."

I arch an eyebrow and smirk. "Think you can?"

"Please, don't make me do this."

I take a step towards him.

He blinks, a slow, syrup-coated blink. "I'm sorry." He flexes his fingers. "*Lux percutiens.*"

A whip crack echoes off the walls and a jagged orb of purple light leaps from Christian's fingers. The sphere darts toward me, heading straight for my heart.

I evade the witch-strike. It whizzes past me, and explodes against the wall in a shower of bright purple sparks. "Close, but no cigar."

He fires again.

My spine bends back, back, back, and the witch-strike sails over my head.

My palms find the floor and I execute a perfect back-flip, landing in a firm stance with ease.

Christian prepares to cast a third time.

I rush forwards, elbow him in the stomach. He crumples to the floor and I plant a foot on his chest. "I'm done fucking around, Kate. Tell me who he is and where he is, or your protégé dies."

"I'll never tell you."

"I wasn't finished. I should've said, your protégé dies...*first*. Then your husband. Then your daughter. And after that, well, I'll go after anyone else you might love."

"You're bluffing," she says, but there's a tremor in her voice.

"Oh, Kate. We both know that's not true. Poor, poor Sally. Seems a shame. She's got such a promising life ahead of her."

Kate's expression hardens. "Fuck you."

"I'll make sure you're there when I do it, too."

She blanches. "Stop this."

"Only you can stop it. If you don't, you *will* watch your daughter die."

"I said stop."

"And I'll make it slow. I'll make sure you hear her scream."

"All right, stop, I'll tell you."

Christian coughs, a sound like stone grating against stone. "No, Kate, don't—"

I lean more weight onto my foot.

Christian's squeals assault my ears.

"Charlie O'Hara." Kate spits the words at me. "His name is Charlie O'Hara. He has a flat on the High Street, Waverly House, number 3B."

"There." I lift my foot off Christian's chest. "That wasn't so hard, was it?"

Christian makes a wheezing sound.

I snap my fingers at Kate. "Car keys, now."

"What?"

"Keys."

"They're still in my bag."

"Get them."

She winces. "My arm."

"Tsk, tsk, tsk. You must think I was born yesterday." I crouch down, grab Christian's head to hold it still, and position my claw right over his eyeball.

He goes completely still.

"What are you doing?" Kate shrieks.

I sigh. This is getting boring. "It's obvious. The minute I leave his side, you'll attack me. Now, stop fucking about and get me the keys, or you'll be helping Christian pick out a glass eye."

Kate stumbles to the spot where her handbag lies on its side, lifts it up with her good hand, and roots through its contents. She draws out her keys.

"Throw them to me."

She does as I ask.

In one fluid motion, I snatch the keys from the air, stoop down, grab a fistful of Christian's shirt and drag him to his feet. "You're driving."

His eyes narrow to slits. "Like hell I am."

"Do you have a death wish?"

Kate clears her throat. "You've got what you wanted. Now let him go."

"Do I look stupid? He's my insurance policy. As long as he's with me, you won't tell any of your MID buddies about this. And if you do decide to tell anyone, or call for backup, or try and stop me in any way..." I draw my finger across my throat.

Christian twists in my grasp, but I hold him tight. "Don't listen to her. She's bluffing. She won't hurt me."

I laugh, another of those sour, humourless laughs. "Guess again."

Kate bites her lip. "I don't have a choice. Go with her."

"But—"

"That's an order, DI Winter."

He clenches his jaw and gives a brief nod.

I slap the keys into his palm and hustle him towards the car. "Get in."

Christian glares at me. "Fine." He jabs a button on the key fob and the car's lights flash. Then he opens the driver's side door, climbs in and slams it shut behind him.

I crouch down beside Kate. "Where are your iron cuffs?"

"Clipped to my belt."

I flick the hem of her jacket aside and snatch the silver-plated cuffs—glimmering under the fluorescent lights—off her belt. A thin band of dull iron—toxic to witches—coats the inner edge. "Good girl."

"You won't get away with this."

"Whatever you say." I yank the door open and slide into the passenger seat. "Put these on, one around your wrist, one around the steering wheel."

Christian's jaw works, but he does as he's told. The cuffs ratchet into place with the sound of metal on metal.

I shoot Kate one long, murderous look. "Remember what I said about calling in back up."

She gulps. "I won't call anyone, I swear. Just don't hurt him."

I close my door and turn to Christian, a wide smile plastered across my face. "Time to pay Charlie-boy a visit."

CHAPTER 8

Kate's *Audi* screeches to a halt outside Waverley House—a run-down tower block that slumps to one side, drunk and dirty-faced, with uneven, blue-grey blinds half-covering the grimy windows like droopy eyelids. The early morning sunlight doesn't improve things. Quite the opposite, in fact. The orange-yellow glow gives the shambling structure a jaundiced, haunted air.

My chest tightens, my shoulders hugging my ears. The day I left home; I swore I'd never set foot in another place like this. "What a shithole."

Christian cuts the ignition and shifts in his seat. "Kate never should've told you about O'Hara. The witness protection program—"

"*What?* So, not only were you shielding Maria's murderer from me, you've given him a new life as what... some kind of reward for killing her?"

He doesn't answer my question. Instead, he says, "You don't have to do this."

I scratch an eyebrow with a hooked talon. "Yeah. I kind of do."

"You're sick. You need help."

I roll my eyes. "Please. I need you to shut the fuck up."

He leans back, propping his head against the headrest, and the anti-magic cuffs clink when he moves. "Think about what's going to happen afterwards, after you've killed him."

"I don't care what happens."

"You should." He twists to face me. "Kate won't ever let this go, and then what, you spend the rest of your life in hiding? If you do this, you'll be shunned. You'll never be part of the witching community again. Where will you go? Where will you live... on the streets?"

"Humph. Wouldn't be the first time."

"What?"

"Nothing."

"I didn't know you used to be homeless."

I shrug, let my gaze drift out of the window and wish I hadn't. Waverly House leers at me with heavy hooded eyes and a dull ache—a phantom pain, the memory of pain, caused by my wonderful Mum—spreads up my arm. The open fracture had taken weeks to heal, the surgical site itching like a mother-fucker, the plates and screws weighing heavy. "I don't care what happens to me. Without Maria, my life's over, anyway."

"That's bullshit, and you know it."

"Is it?"

Christian's eyes are so dark that it's hard to work out where the iris ends and the pupil begins, exactly the same shade as Maria's. People always used to think they were related, but they aren't.

Weren't.

My stomach twinges, but it's muted and far-off.

"I miss her too." His voice sounds small.

"Don't."

"I know how much she loved you."

"Shut up."

"She wasn't the only one. You have friends who love you. Kate loves you. I love you. Isn't that enough?"

"For fuck's sake." I snort. "Have you been binge watching *Buffy the Vampire Slayer* again?"

"What are you—"

"Let me be crystal clear." My hand closes around his throat. "I'm not Dark Willow and you're not Xander. I don't need your love, or your pity, and I sure as hell don't need some knight in soppy armour to save me."

His face turns pink, then red, then purple under my grip. "Tally—stop—not too late."

I squeeze harder and his words choke off. "You don't get it, do you? I gave into this because I couldn't handle the pain of losing her. You think I'd ever want to feel that again?" I release him.

He coughs and splutters.

A flash of movement catches my eye.

The man who trudges along the High Street, towards Waverley House, trains his gaze on the floor and keeps his hands behind his back. I wouldn't have spotted him later in the day, in the crowded rush of the city. He has one of those faces, the kind you forget seconds after meeting him, and his clothes are plain, all muted colours—grey and beige.

My lips purse and I narrow my eyes. "Is that him?"

Christian makes a noise in his throat, but he doesn't answer.

I grab his wrist and squeeze.

Bones crack, and he cries out.

"Answer the question."

"Yes." Christian's voice is high and strangled.

"Good." I peel my fingers off his skin, open the door and climb out of the car. Winking at Christian, I incline my head towards the iron cuffs shackling him to the steering wheel and my mouth quirks at the corner. "Don't go anywhere."

"Don't be stupid, you can't—"

I slam the door, Christian already forgotten, tracking Charlie's path along the street. This is him. This is the man who murdered Maria, this blander than vanilla wet weekend. My claws bite into my palms, but I welcome the pain.

Charlie shoots a friendly smile at a passer-by and bobs his head at them. "Morning."

A chink of doubt wheedles its way in, insidious and painful, like a lit cigarette to the temple. Charlie seems... nice.

Maybe I'm wrong.

Maybe he isn't all bad.

No.

Remember what he did, remember what you've lost, remember Maria.

The doubt fades, replaced with a cold certainty.

Charlie O'Hara is going to die today.

He reaches the entrance to Waverly House and punches a code into the keypad on the main door. A loud beep sounds, a green light flashes, and he wrenches the door open.

"Charlie O'Hara." My voice is loud in the dawn silence.

He tries to keep his face blank, but I notice his reaction to me—the wide eyes, the puckered lips. He gives me the same smile he gave the passer-by, sweet enough to rot my teeth. "Can I help you?"

"You killed my wife."

"I'm sorry, but you're mistaken."

"Don't fucking lie to me." I unfurl my fingers, my talons glinting.

Charlie's face pales and he holds out his hands, palms facing me. "Why do you think I murdered your wife?"

"Maria." The word catches in my throat.

"Oh." His mouth tugs down at the corners. "You're Talitha. The MID told me about you after..."

"Bingo."

He shakes his head, and his eyes glisten. "I didn't know what I was doing. Someone mesmerised me. I don't remember any of it, and—"

"You did it. It was you, and now, you're going to pay."

"You need to listen to me—"

"Listen to you? I need to kill you."

His brow creases. "Kill me? I..." His expression clears. "Oh, Jesus. You're a—a—"

"A Fury." I start towards him.

He bolts inside and slams the door.

I sigh.

He's a fool if he thinks he can escape me.

I stomp across the road, my heavy footsteps echoing off the surrounding buildings. When I reach the door, I grab the handle and pull, my muscles straining until the locking mechanism snaps and I tear the door open. I stalk down a narrow hallway with peeling wallpaper until I reach a dingy staircase.

Charlie races up the stairs, taking them two at a time.

"You can't run from me." I place my foot on the first step.

He fires a spell at me.

I duck back.

The spell takes a chunk out of the wall.

I step on to the staircase again.

His head twists in my direction and he trips, his legs flying out from under him.

I climb to the second step.

He clambers to his feet. "Stay away from me."

I'm on the third step, my heart slamming against my rib cage. "We can do this the easy way or the fun way."

He bounds to the top of the staircase, the sole of his shoe squeaking on the cracked floorboards as he pivots and disappears around a corner.

"The fun way it is."

I'm in no rush, so I take my sweet, sweet time. The stairs creak beneath my weight and, as I climb, I trail my claws along the wall, the filthy paper flaking away like dead skin. I emerge on the first-floor landing.

Charlie vanishes around another corner and races up a second set of stairs. He's panting, breaths exploding from him in heavy gasps.

I whistle as I stroll down the hallway, still scraping away the soiled wallpaper with my claws.

He's on the third-floor landing already, his footsteps pounding over my head for another few seconds before they stop. He must have reached his flat.

I'm halfway up the second staircase when Charlie's key scrapes in the lock, followed by the sound of rushed footsteps and a door slamming. I spin on my heel at the top of the staircase.

Two doors, both red, paint peeling, face each other. A window—thick with grime—turns the light a milky brown. The sickly glow leeches through and glimmers off the plaques fixed to the doors.

3A and 3B.

I reach out, my fingers inches from the door to 3B when they brush against something hard, unyielding and invisible.

A witch-weave—a spell designed to keep other witches out.

But I'm not a witch anymore.

In one of the stories I heard, they even have this super-powerful scream that can blast through objects... and even spells.

"That won't keep you safe," I say. The same sharp pain I felt back at the house builds in my stomach and rises in my chest and my throat.

The Fury's scream.

It builds and builds and builds—

3A's door squeaks open and a woman in her mid-thirties steps out of the flat. She has dirty blonde hair—scraped back into a high ponytail—massive gold hoops swing from her earlobes, and she smacks a piece of gum with her mouth open. She rakes her eyes over me, from head to toe. Takes in my white hair, my ghost-pale skin and black claws. "You know Halloween's next week, right?" She rolls her eyes, blows a bubble with the gum and pops it with her tongue. "What are you supposed to be, anyway?"

"Fuck off."

"Oi, twat features." She gets in my face, and I'm assaulted by the bittersweet stench of mint, stale cigarette smoke, and two-week-old bacon fat—the scent of my *perfect* childhood.

My mother smelled the same on the day it happened.

The break.

Mint.

Stale cigarette smoke.

Two-week-old bacon fat.

The memory comes unbidden.

I'm fourteen, lying on my bed, *The Kaiser Chiefs* belting out Highroyds through the speakers...

CHAPTER 9

BEFORE MARIA

The radio is loud, but Mum's moans and groans—and those of her afternoon client—still echo through the wafer-thin walls. I get up, whack the volume up to full blast, and launch myself back onto the bed. Seconds later, the door bursts open.

Mum barges in, red-faced and sweating—a leopard print kimono fastened at her waist, and a cloud of white powder dusting her upper lip. "Turn that fucking shit off, I'm trying to work."

I turn my head away. "Is that what you call it?"

"What did you say?"

"You heard me."

"Turn. It. Off."

"Make me."

"Right." She lunges at me, grabs a fistful of my hair and yanks me to my feet.

Pain explodes over my scalp, and I squeal, lashing out with hooked fingers. I claw at her face, drawing blood and rip away from her. I scream as a chunk of my hair comes out in her clenched fist.

She clutches at her cheek, blood dripping between her fingers. "You little cunt."

"Fat old slag." I stride across the room and shove her out of the way.

"Where do you think you're going, lady?"

"Out."

"Get back here now."

"I'd tell you to get fucked, but I think you've got that covered."

I'm at the top of the stairs when I get a waft of it.

Mint.

Stale cigarette smoke.

Two-week-old bacon fat.

Mum's bony hands slam into my back, and I pitch forward, shrieking. I tumble down the stairs, the world somersaulting over and over and over. Agony rips through my entire body and—

Snap.

My arm goes numb. I crash to the hall floor in a heap, open my eyes—my arm, stretched out in front of me, juts out at a crooked angle and a shard of bone peeks through the skin. I pass out then, but not before I'm saturated in that malign stench.

Mint.

Stale cigarette smoke.

Two-week-old bacon fat.

CHAPTER 10

NOW

T he same stink that saturates me now.

"You deaf, or what?" The woman from 3A says. "I don't know who you think you are, barging in here with your shitty wig, and your fucking attitude but—"

I twist, jam my forearm against her collarbone, and drive her back. Her shoulder blades slam into the window and a crack appears in the glass. "You can leave through the front door, or the window, I don't care which." I release her.

She stares back at me, slack-jawed, the off-white wad of chewing gum stuck to one of her off-white teeth.

She's disgusting.

I could kill her...

No.

Fun as it would be, I'm not here for her.

I'm here for Charlie-boy.

"Go on then. Off you fuck." I wave my fingers in a shoeing motion.

She scrambles past me and darts for the stairs, shoes clattering on the wooden floor.

I pivot on my heel so I'm facing 3B again and strain my ears. My heightened senses pick up the sound of ragged breathing from behind the door. "Little pig, little pig, let me in."

The tempo of the panting increases and Charlie's footsteps scurry away, retreating deeper into the flat.

"Or I'll huff and I'll puff." I take a deep breath, open my mouth wide and scream. The window—and the light bulb in the ceiling—shatters and glass rains down. A barrage of shimmering energy waves surge from my mouth and slam into the door. The frame splinters, and the door flies off its hinges and crashes to the floor.

A blanket of silence falls.

I stride through the empty frame, over the fallen door and into Charlie's flat, which is open plan—grey carpet tiles, a faded sofa with frayed stitching, a cramped kitchenette—with a huge sash window letting the light pour in. The flat appears empty.

I slink around the edge of the room, close my eyes, and listen.

Thud-thud, thud-thud, thud-thud.

"I know you're in here, Charlie-boy. I can hear your heart beating. You're scared, aren't you? You should be."

Thud-thud-thud, thud-thud-thud, thud-thud-thud.

I open my eyes, head snapping round. "Quit playing hide and seek, *witch*." I squint my fury-enhanced eyes. A slightly darker patch of magnolia—in the shape of a man—hugs one wall.

Charlie's tried to cloak himself beneath an invisibility spell.

I let my lips curve into a wicked grin. "Found you." I take a step towards him.

The air around the man-shaped imprint ripples like droplets of water on a puddle, and the static buzz of magic prickles through the room.

Charlie reappears and flings out a hand. "*Confinium.*"

Ropes of white light spring from his fingers and shoot towards me, wrapping around my torso and pinning my arms to my sides. I struggle against the ropes. "You'll regret that." They slacken a little.

Charlie flexes his wrist, and the ropes tighten again and bite into my skin. He slides a phone from his pocket.

"What the hell are you doing?"

"Phoning the MID."

"No." If he calls the MID, they'll send officers by portal. Maybe more than I can handle. The limits of my new powers are an unknown quantity, and I don't want to test them. I strain against the ropes, the muscles in my arms burning. I strain harder and the ropes snap.

Charlie drops the phone, and it clatters to the floor. "-*Mortem*." A death-strike flashes into his hand, hissing and spitting. He launches it at me and it screams through the air.

I bat the spell away with my hand.

It doesn't even phase me.

The white light careens into the window and it smashes, the glass blasting outward.

I dart forward before Charlie can make another move, grab a fistful of his shirt and hoist him up, so that his feet dangle off the floor. "Time for you to pay."

He kicks my shins as I step across to the window, using all his strength, but the kicks feel like puffs of air against my legs. "Please, let me go. Please."

Kate's car is across the street. Christian stares up at us through the windscreen, struggling against the cuffs that bind him to the steering wheel. His mouth opens and closes and I can tell he's shouting. He yanks and twists and wrenches, but it's no use.

I raise an eyebrow at Charlie. "You want me to let you go?"

"Ye—yes."

I take two steps forward, so that his legs swing out of the window. "Whatever you say."

His eyes bulge and an inhuman howl tears through his lips. A dark stain spreads down his trouser leg.

My face scrunches up. "Disgusting."

"No, no, no." He clutches my arm and grips so tight the tips of his fingers turn purple. "Please."

"This," I say, "is for Maria."

"Wait—"

I thrust my arm out and release him.

The world slows down.

Charlie's body arcs high into the air and hangs there, and hangs there, and hangs there, suspended in nothingness. Then he falls and falls and keeps on falling. His screams echo all the way down and I drink them in. Charlie lands, with a loud crash, on the bonnet of Kate's car—the metalwork crumpling—his body bounces, his arms flopping out to the sides. He doesn't move after that, save for a trickle of blood that dribbles from the corner of his lip.

I stare into his blank, empty eyes. A slow, rictus grin peels my lips away from my teeth.

Christian's still shouting, his face scarlet, and his wrist is bleeding where the cuff has sliced into it.

I don't care, because it's done.

I've avenged Maria's death.

I'd expected an enormous surge of victory, a sweeping tide of relief, something—*anything*—but there's nothing there.

No, wait.

There's one thing.

Fury.

Cold, boiling fury, and nothing more.

Can I Ask You a Cheeky Favour?

Thanks for reading *The Fury's Vengeance* and joining Tally on her quest to avenge Maria's death. I hope you enjoyed the book.

Reviews are really important to authors. They help other readers—like you—discover our work.

If you liked the book, and have a couple of minutes to spare, it would be great if you could leave a short, honest review on the book's Amazon or Goodreads page.

Happy reading!

Cheers

Shane

want more from the MYTH & Magic universe?

DOWNLOAD YOUR EXCLUSIVE PREQUEL SHORT STORY, THE THIEF'S MAGIC (MYTH & MAGIC, BOOK 0.5), FOR FREE!

If someone you love was suffering, how far would you go to save them?

Want to read Geek's origin story and follow his journey to COVEN?

You can download The Thief's Magic (Myth & Magic, Book 0.5) today!

Visit: https://bit.ly/thethiefsmagic

ACKNOWLEDGMENTS

First, foremost, and always, thank you to my family and friends for your unwavering encouragement and support. You guys rock!

To my epic editor, Alexa Padou from *Luna Imprints Author Services*, thank you for another brilliant edit. Your passion for improving my work and rounding out my characters is truly inspiring. Here's to working on many more books together.

Thank you to Damon and the team at *Damonza* for another fantastic book cover. Just like with my other protagonists, you brought Tally to life, and I couldn't be more grateful.

To my author mentors, I'm in awe of your talent, generosity, and expertise. You know who you are.

To all the writers I know (whether that be on Instagram, or from the Rebel Author, Next Level Authors, and Dialogue Doctor *Patreon* communities), I can't thank you enough. I won't name individuals (because I *will* miss someone out and feel bad about it), but you are my people, and the author journey is much easier because of you.

As always—and last but by no means least—a thousand thank yous to my readers. It astounds me that people want to read my words. I am honoured and humbled by your continued support.

ABOUT THE AUTHOR

S. W. Millar is the author of the *Myth & Magic* urban fantasy thriller series. He is also a *Fictionary Certified StoryCoach*, and is currently working on a series of craft guides for writers.

Shane holds a BA in journalism and is a member of *The Alliance of Independent Authors (ALLi)*. He lives in Buckinghamshire, England.

He has taken too many writing courses to count and enjoys reading as much as possible. Shane is obsessed with five things: the writing craft, mythology, personal development, food, and martial arts movies.

Connect with Shane on Instagram

https://www.instagram.com/swmillarauthor/

Visit Shane's Website

https://swmillar.com

ALSO BY S. W. MILLar

Myth & Magic

The Thief's Magic # 0.5 (FREE prequel short story)
The Witch's Revenge # 1
The Coven's Executioner # 2
The Demon's Shadow # 4 (out in May 2022)
More *Myth & Magic* coming soon...

Printed in Great Britain
by Amazon